TEN FACTS YOU MIGHT NOT KNOW ABOUT PLUTO

1. Pluto's first settler was called Flumpenslurp Blurble. Yes, Flumpenslurp Blurble. No wonder she had to leave Earth for somewhere new. Luckily, everyone's welcome on Pluto.

2. The biggest animals on Pluto are blue-headed skwitches which are ten-foot-tall birds with spaghetti legs. Try not to be kidnapped by one. I was and it's not as fun as it sounds.

3. Pluto was once covered in smelly vomblefruit trees and no one wanted to visit it. Now it has one tourist — me!

4. The best place on the whole of Pluto is Doolybop-pers Café where my friend Straxi lives with her twin, Bryd. Their mum and dad serve amazing food like Whirlywangs, Blobble Burgers, Bugglecrumpets and Ri

Tentacles.

5. The Glowing Canyon and Blue Prairies are beautiful places to visit.

6. The Pulsating Swamp is not. The kindest thing to say about it is that it was a big mistake. Unfortunately it's been left to get even bigger.

7. Snarglers are blind, double-ended slug things that live in the Pulsating Swamp. For a lot of people on Pluto they are entertainment.

8. The President of Pluto likes to set competitions. They often go wrong like the Pulsating Swamp. He still likes to do them.

9. I won a competition to write these facts for the Pluto Tourist Board.

10. I don't think I'll be asked to do it again.

Jon Fisher

INVITATION

Doris Fisher and President Jim Clyde

invite you to celebrate their wedding

On Happyday 2nd of Darwin 2317

as they bungee jump off the Vertigo Hotel

while saying their vows

Followed by gravity-free party in

the Pop-up Ballroom

RSVP ASAP

THE SOLAR TIMES

Pluto edition

MISSING SNARGLER

A snargler has gone missing from the Pulsating Swamp, according to the Snargler Spotters' Society. "I myself have personally counted them using my official Snargler Spotters' Notebook (Gold Member edition) and there is definitely one missing," said Chief Spotter Eugene Nerdlington. "If anyone spots it, please return it to the swamp before it dries out." When asked to describe the missing snargler, Eugene could only say it was similar in shape and size to a sausage. All citizens are asked to check their barbecues before using them, just in case.

SPECIAL SUNSET TONIGHT

The President has left instructions for a special sunset tonight to celebrate the beginning of his honey-moon.
According to the President, "Oranges and reds will intermingle with a soft pinky haze to produce a romantic glow over the horizon – as long as I have programmed in the right instructions." Citizens are asked not to get their hopes up. Chance of migraine today: high

PRESIDENT HAS EXTREME WEDDING

The President of Pluto got hitched in style yesterday when he and his bride leapt from the roof of the Vertigo Hotel on the end of bungee ropes. "It was perfect," said the presi--dent's new wife Doris, who comes from Earth. "And to think I might not even have visited Pluto if it hadn't been for my grandson. Thanks, Jon!"

Due to an error in timing, Doris was bouncing up just as the President was jumping down. "We had to shout our vows to each other as we passed but it was fine," said Doris. "It was certainly a wedding to remember," commented celebrant Boogle Bopton, hastily unsnapping his safety harness and vomit--ing into a pongle bush.

While the happy couple honeymoon on Saturn, Pluto will be run by the winner of the 'Fancy Running Pluto While I'm Away Then Why Not Enter This Competition' competition: Mrs Hall. Mrs Hall is a teacher from Earth who has lots of ideas about how to improve Pluto. I'm sure everyone here on Pluto wishes her the best of luck. She'll need it.

LIKE NOT KNOWING WHICH WAY IS UP?

Then why not become a Gravity Guy? Learn the latest moves while making sure no one floats away on Pluto. Get with it and join them today! Training and motion sickness pills provided.

The Fishers

Northcroft Road

England

Earth

Dear Jon,

I know I said this to you before we left you on
Pluto, but you were too busy eating Whirlywangs
to listen so I've written it down.

Please cut round the dotted lines and stick it to
the wall by your bed.

D
L

(cut out and stick to wall)

WHILE YOU ARE ON PLUTO REMEMBER TO:

✹ Brush your teeth

✹ Change your underpants

✹ Wear your gravity medal so you don't

float away

✹ Brush your teeth

✹ Do what Mr and Mrs Dooly ask you to

✹ Work hard at Flumpenslurp Blurble School

✹ Brush your teeth

I'm so glad Mrs Hall has asked you to carry on writing letters.

Dad says be good and don't get snatched by any more skwitches.

Love Mum & Dad

PS Don't forget to brush your teeth.

Dawn's Lawns jobs
- Cut own lawn – urgent!
- Design scented garden for old folks' home
- See Mrs Thompson re hedges

Doolyboppers

Dizzy Street

Dome 1

Pluto

Dear Mum,

I have brushed my teeth.

Thank you for letting me stay on

Pluto with Straxi a bit longer.

It's weird here now

you've all gone home.

I feel very far away.

And I am. Seven

and a half billion kilometres.

I wish Mrs Hall was that far away. I never thought my teacher would follow me all the way to Pluto. She's still going on at me to be the face of her handwriting campaign.

"Can't I stop now?" I asked, but no, her mission to get everyone writing will never end. Maybe now she's won the competition to run Pluto for a month she will be too busy?

I can't wait to start at Flumpenslurp
Blurble School, as they do weird

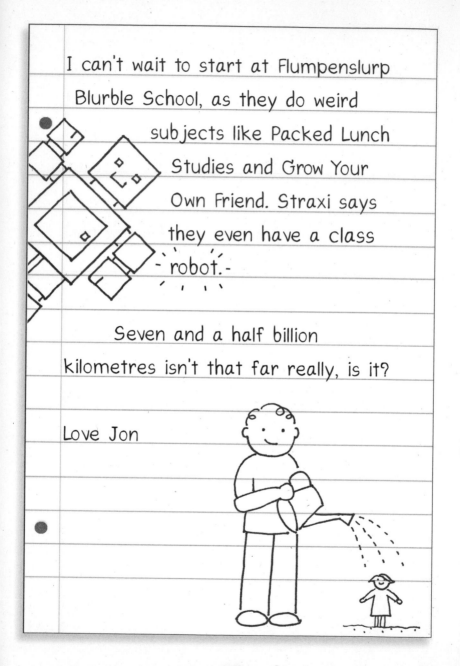

subjects like Packed Lunch
Studies and Grow Your
Own Friend. Straxi says
they even have a class
robot.

Seven and a half billion
kilometres isn't that far really, is it?

Love Jon

Northcroft Road

Earth

Dear Jon,

You said you brushed your teeth, but you didn't
say when? Please add the words 'EVERY DAY' to
your list.

Remember you can come home any time you want.

Don't tell him that! - big bruv

Our flight back to Earth was a bit quieter than
on the way out. I wonder why? Your little sis
cried because she missed Fiona the Feathery
Pony and told everyone on board (the crew

D
L

basically) all about how she was kidnapped by a blue-headed skwitch and flew on its back and made it her friend.

She only stopped crying when the co-pilot let her dress him up as a skwitch and make him a nest out of towels. She said he enjoyed it but I'm sure I heard him say 'Help!' a few times in a strangled voice through his cardboard beak.

When we got home, the garden had grown into a jungle and I had to spend all day hacking through it because it was a really bad advertisement for Dawn's Lawns.

Meanwhile, Dad's pile of broken computers waiting to be mended was touching the ceiling. He was delighted.

Your big brother Jason is acting very strangely. He is creeping about the house peering behind the furniture and writing things in a notebook. It reminds me of when we went snargler spotting on Pluto.

I'm so glad I didn't spot any of those disgusting creatures. At least the slugs on Earth are small and only have one end.

Gran has sent us a postcard from Saturn — did

you get one?

Love Mum & Dad

PS   Your little sis has written Fiona a letter so plese can you reed it to her and giv Fiona a big kiss and a hug

Yes all right darling stop writing on my letter I think Jon gets the idea.

D
L

Dear Fiona the
Feathery Pony

I love you

Plese com to Er f you can
fly here wiv your wings
flap flap

Luve from yor very best
frend

Jenny that's me

xxxxxxxxxxx

19

Jon,

Saturn is awesome! The first thing we did was hire flying pods and go racing round the rings. The organisers say I'm a natural and want me to enter the Saturn Ring Race. Qualifiers start tomorrow! Guess I'll have to get my revenge on the blarb-ringed flapper on Neptune another time. Got to go – time for our abseiling lesson.

Gran x

Jon Fisher

c/o The Doolys

Doolyboppers

Dizzy Street

Dome 1

Pluto

Pan

Hi Gran,

Good luck in the qualifiers.

Hope you get through!

What should I call the President now you've married him? These are the options: Jim, Grandad Jim, Grandad President, President Grandad, President Grandad Jim or Grandad President Jim.

Jon x

Gran ~~Fisher~~ I mean Clyde

Flabber Flotel

Ring Street

D Ring

Saturn

If you **LOVE** pod racing, why not try the Ultimate Pod Racing Experience:

THE SATURN RING RACE

Anyone can enter this open competition, but be warned: there's **DANGER** at every twist and turn.

Can you stay in orbit?
Can you stay on the track? Will you make it through the heats to become the

SATURN RING RACE CHAMPION?

Qualifiers start from Pandora moon in F ring tomorrow

Doolyboppers

Pluto

Dear Mum,

Straxi and I went to see the
skwitches to give Fiona the Feathery
Pony her letter from little sis.

They love the modern art sculptures
Straxi's dad designed for their new
nesting places, even though they look
like coat-hangers to me.
The sculptures I mean,
not the skwitches.

coat hanger ♪

The vomblefruit tree that
Straxi and I helped to save
is growing pretty big now,
but not big enough to hold a
skwitch's nest yet or even
one of their tail feathers
which Straxi has measured
and found to be the length
of one dad.

skwitch

We looked for Fiona the FP and
Armitage Shanks in the
forest of skwitch legs. It
was like being trapped in a
packet of spaghetti.

Straxi said don't worry, they will come
up to us as they are now our friends.

I said Armitage kidnapped us just a
few weeks ago so maybe he's not
such a great friend after all but
Straxi said he couldn't help it and
that he was confused.

We found them and guess what? They
are building a nest together!
Straxi says they will
have lots of
baby blue-
headed

skwitches and I will be an uncle. She is > mad. <

Mrs Hall has officially taken over as Temporary President of Pluto for the month and has already made some new laws. They are just like school rules.

I don't think Mrs Hall knows how to run a planet.

"Don't worry about it. Just be a skwitch," Straxi said. So I stood on one leg. But I made sure I didn't stand near Armitage, just in case he decided to kidnap me again.

Love Jon

PS Here is a photo of Fiona the FP for little sis. It was the best we could get.

NEW PLUTO LAWS

· There will be a whole-planet assembly every morning in the Town Square in Dome 1. Meet by the statue of Flumpenslurp Blurble's spaceship.

· Penpals will be given to everyone.

· The person who writes the best letter each week gets to take home the school cactus.

· People dropping litter will be given detention.

M. Hall

Signed Mrs Hall, Temporary President

SPECIAL EMERGENCY BULLETIN

Fiveday 30 Darwin 2317

Dear members,

You will be alarmed to hear of the disappearance of Snargler 192 from the Pulsating Swamp.

As you know, Snargler 192 is a very special snargler as he is a rare Middle Swamp snargler and thus particularly interesting, even more interesting than the Northern or Southern Swamp snargler if that is possible.

All members are asked to gather at the Pulsating Swamp on Funday so that we can form a line and search the area. Here is a recent photo of Snargler 192 for identification purposes.

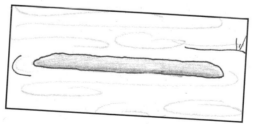

Eugene Nerdlington, Chief Snargler Spotter

Northcroft Road

Earth

Dear Jon,

I gave the photo of Fiona the Feathery Pony to your sister. She has put it under her pillow. Here is another letter for Fiona. Please can you read it to her

and dont just mak up the words lik Mummy dos in my bedtim story wen she is tyred or I will no

Yes ok darling stop taking my pen.

Love Mum & Dad

PS   You should brush for at least two minutes -
I forgot to put that in the letter. You will
remember, won't you?

Dawn's Lawns jobs

✔ Cut lawn in front of library

✔ Design sensory garden for nursery

✔ Trim Mrs Thompson's hedge into
                              dove!!!
   shape of ~~glove~~

Dear Fiona the
Fethery Pony

If you fly to Erf we can
hav a sleep ova and put on
nayl varnish

I hav writ you a peom
I am on Erf
You are on Pluto
That is reely noying

Luve from yor very best
frend
Jenny that's me
xxxxxxxxxxx

Jon,

I won my race and I'm through to
the next round! Epic! Grandad
President Jim is buying me a
second-hand racing pod. It's a bit
battered but at least I've got my
own now. Can't wait to try it out at
the next heat tomorrow.

Got to go – caving expedition about
to start.

Gran x

Jon Fisher
c/o The Doolys
Doolyboppers
Dizzy Street
Dome 1
Pluto

Epimetheus

33

Hi Gran,

Good luck in the next round.

Now that you have your own pod

you'll be brilliant!

It's pretty quiet here and so far

only <u>one</u> thing has escaped.

I bet President Grandad Jim will

be relieved to hear that.

Jon x

Gran Fisher-Clyde

Flabber Flotel

Ring Street

D Ring

Saturn

Doolyboppers

Dizzy Street

Dome 1

Pluto

Dear Mum

Turns out those lessons I told you
about are actually called Friendship
Studies and Grow Your Own Packed
Lunch. But they were still good.

We were allowed to create our own
plants, so Straxi and I made a potato
crisp tree.

The flavour will be **✳** sugar lumps and scampi.

The class robot helped make the flavour by mixing an artificial smell. It was so strong the whole school had to be evacuated. After we were allowed back in, we had Friendship Studies and there was a special guest.

"Get ready to be excited!" said Mrs Urdlepun, the class teacher, but I don't know why she said that as it was Mrs Hall who stood in front of us and announced that she was my teacher from Earth. She then told us all about letter writing and said I was the 'face' of her campaign and I wanted to disappear as usual.

But actually it wasn't bad as we got to talk all about how Straxi and I saved Pluto with our letters and how we sent the vomblefruit to Pluto so it could grow again. I felt really proud and got ready for the class to lift me up on their shoulders like a

hero but no one did as they were too
busy being given penpals of their own.

Mrs Hall is giving all the adults on
Pluto penpals too. She says it will help
the community spirit.

Spirit? "Great, I love ghosts," I said,
and pretended to be one for the rest
of the lesson, drifting about
and going,

"Whoooooooo!"

"Good luck with him," Mrs Hall
said to Mrs Urdlepun as she left.

Bryd has to write to someone in Dome 3 called Opuntia Microdasys. She spent the rest of the day trying to spell their name. Mr Dooly has been told he has to write to his next door neighbour. At least it will save on postage and give him a chance to borrow a cup of furgel powder if he ever runs out.

Love Jon

PS I have more teeth than Straxi. Do I need to brush the extra ones or just leave them as they are spares?

Northcroft Road

Earth

Dear Jon,

HELP! There's a snargler loose in the house!

It turns out Jason smuggled it home from Pluto in
his hood and then promptly lost it as soon as he
walked in. That's why he was creeping about with
a notebook - he was snargler spotting!

Well I wish he'd found it. It could be anywhere.
Dad says it could be crawling up my leg while I'm
writing this letter. Yes thank you dear, that's
really helpful.

How do you track down a missing snargler?

Please ask Straxi ASAP!

Love Mum & Dad

PS Dad says there is no such thing as spare teeth, unless you are a shark.

Dawn's Lawns jobs

✔ Cut lawn in front of post office
✔ Design aquatic garden for Fish Keepers' Society
✔ Trim Mrs Thompson's other hedge into shape of ~~beer~~ deer!!!

Doolyboppers, the best café on Pluto

Dizzy Street

Dome 1

Pluto

Dear Mr and Mrs Fisher,

Straxi here! Jon says you have a snargler loose in your house. I wish I did.

Anyway, I went to see the Chief Snargler Spotter, Eugene Nerdlington, to get his advice. He was very glad to hear that Snargler 192 is ok but also very worried as it has never travelled in space before. Or travelled before. Or done anything before. It has only lain in the bottom of a swamp. So everything will be new and strange. Here's what he said to do.

1. DO NOT PANIC.

2. Well, panic just a little bit but don't let the snargler notice.

3. Above all, keep the snargler calm. No one knows what happens when a snargler freaks out, as no snargler has ever freaked out before.

4. Here's how to catch it. Snarglers like to live in groups, so all you have to do is

all lie on the floor pretending to be snarglers and it will come out and join you. Just lie on the floor staring at the ceiling. It isn't hard - I do it all the time. (Me, not Chief Snargler Spotter Eugene Nerdlington, although maybe he does it at home when no one's looking.)

5. After a while the snargler should come and join you. It moves slowly so you should be able to catch it during the hour or two it takes to move across the floor.

lie on the floor
like this

Here is a diagram. Good luck!

Love Straxi

PS Here is a snargler care fact sheet for
you to read.

PPS And I've made some snargler
outfits for you all!

SNARGLER
CARE FACT SHEET

Snargler Spotters' Society

Snarglers should <u>never</u> be kept as pets.

These fascinating creatures deserve the freedom to lie motionless at the bottom of swamps all day, as campaigned for by the Society for Snarglers Lying On the Bottom of Swamps or S.L.O.B.S.. However if you do find yourself caring for a lost or injured snargler before returning it to its natural habitat, these guidelines should help.

Create the right environment
Snarglers naturally live in the Pulsating Swamp so try to find a habitat that is as similar as possible. You can create a swamp using mud, water and bicarbonate of soda. Some people may find a similar environment at the back of the fridge.

Offer suitable foods
Snarglers eat swamp mites which are so small they are invisible, and scientists can only guess they exist by the fact that snarglers are alive. This makes catching swamp mites extremely difficult, and if you do catch them you won't know you have. You may even have one now. See? Difficult, isn't it? Try a popular hooped breakfast cereal instead.

Swamp mite magnified 1000 times

Provide enrichment activities

Snarglers may seem like dull, lifeless slugs but we at the Snargler Spotters' Society believe them to be complex, intelligent creatures. A stimulating conversation and a burst of opera music will help your snargler thrive. If, indeed, it actually notices. It may be on a higher plane of existence, or just have wind.

Safety first

Since snarglers resemble sausages, keep them away from puff pastry or baked beans for their own (and your taste buds') safety.

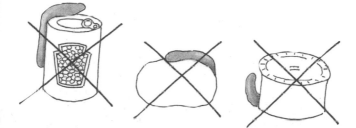

If you have read to the bottom of this fact sheet you must be very interested in snarglers indeed. Have you thought about joining the Snargler Spotters' Society? We love wearing anoraks, drinking plubberslurp from our flasks and writing in our Snargler Spotters' Notebooks. Apply to SSHQ, Pulsating Swamp, Dome 1.

(Also, have you thought about joining the Secret Snargler Spotters' Society, for people who like snarglers but don't want anyone to know? If so, then apply to SSSHQ, Pulsating Swamp, Dome 1. Shhhh!)

Northcroft Road

Earth

Dear Jon,

Well, we tried Straxi's method of catching the snargler. We all lay on the living room floor: me, Dad, Jason and Jenny. Please thank Straxi for the snargler costumes which were very convincing. Dad's was a bit tight but he just about managed to squeeze into it.

We lay there for a while and Jenny sang us a song about sparkly snarglers in the sunset. It seemed like ages.

And then we heard a rustling noise.

"It's Deathray!" said Jason, who has named the snargler.

"It's Sparkly!" said Jenny, who has also named the snargler.

"It's huge!" yelled Dad.

"That's a stupid name," said Jason, and then he turned round and saw what we all saw – a giant grey sausage the size of the neighbour's dog oozing in through the doorway.

"What's happened to Sparkly?" cried Jenny.

"Deathray's mutated! Brilliant!" said Jason.

"Is it supposed to have those massive teeth?" I asked, but nobody was listening as they were all running away. So I joined them. Dad hid us all behind his giant tower of broken computers.

We are still there. I hope you get this letter as I am throwing it out of the window and hoping someone picks it up and posts it.

Love Mum & Dad

Jon,

I can't believe it – I'm through to
the quarter finals! Righteous! As a
wedding present, Grandad President
Jim has bought me a brand new
racing pod. Only a basic SpeedPod
V5 but should get me round
without breaking down. Can't wait
to give it a go!

Got to dash – sky diving starting in
5 mins.

Gran x

Jon Fisher

c/o The Doolys

Doolyboppers

Dizzy Street

Dome 1

Pluto

Calypso

Hi Gran,

Good luck in the quarter finals.

Your new pod will be great!

Mrs Hall is making everyone

write letters to each other. And

the thing that escaped has

grown into a giant but at least

we know where it is. So tell

President GrandJim not to worry

about _anything._

Jon x

Gran Fisher-Clyde

Flabber Flotel

Ring Street

D Ring

Saturn

Doolyboppers

Pluto

Dear Mum,

I hope you, Dad and
Jenny managed to
escape from the giant snargler.
(Not so worried about big bruv.)

I asked the Snargler Spotters'
Society what to do, but it was hard to
get an answer as they were <u>very</u>
excited to learn that Sparkly
Deathray has mutated.

It's so interesting that they have filled their notebooks and started new ones.

Anyway, at last I got them to give me an emergency pop-up snargler carry case to send you so you can send it to me. Just follow the instructions to pop it up. Tip: you put the snargler inside after you've popped it up, not before.

Jon

MORE NEW PLUTO LAWS

• Times tables will be recited every day.

• Spelling tests will take place in the tourist office on Fridays.

• If you are awarded the school cactus for your letter writing, please remember to water it.

• Anyone who commits a crime will miss 5 minutes of golden time.

M.Hall

Signed Mrs Hall, Temporary President

Northcroft Road

Earth

Dear Jon,

We managed to get out from behind the pile of
computers.

The snargler went upstairs and into Jason's
bedroom. Dad ran up and shut the door behind it.
It is now living on crusty odd socks, week-old
bacon sandwiches stuck to their plates and heavy
metal music.

The box you sent is too small. I don't think you

realise how big Sparkly Deathray has grown. We are going to use the one the new frigd-a-dish-a-wash came in. Jenny is excited about Sparkly's journey and has decorated the box with stickers and glitter to make it feel happy.

"I know what will make it happy," said Dad.

"Human flesh."

We all laughed but he was only half joking.

Wish us luck.

Love Mum & Dad

Dawn's Lawns jobs
✓ Cut lawn behind playground
✓ Design Jurassic garden for Junior Dinosaur Club
✓ Order Mrs Thompson's garden gnome

SPECIAL EMERGENCY
BULLETIN
Oneday 23 Gagarin 2318

Dear members,

As you may have heard, Snargler 192 has mutated into a giant.

Should we accept it back into the Pulsating Swamp at the risk of infecting our other snarglers? Will it fit? Should we extend the swamp by allowing it to pulsate over to the other side of the clubhouse?

Please come to a special voting session at the clubhouse tomorrow night, where we will also be giving out more notebooks in case you have filled yours up with all the very interesting news.

I certainly have.

Eugene Nerdlington, Chief Snargler Spotter

Jon,

I'm through to the semi-finals!
Legendary! To celebrate, Grandad
President Jim is upgrading my
SpeedPod V5 to a Turbo-Charged
NitroPod SE. Woo-hoo! Can't
wait to give it a whirl.

Got to go — being interviewed for
Planet-hopping Pensioners
Monthly before extreme skiing
party.

Gran x

Jon Fisher

c/o The Doolys

Doolyboppers

Dizzy Street

Dome 1

Pluto

Phoebe

Hi Gran,

Good luck in the semi-finals. Your NitroPod will smash it! Mrs Hall is now making everyone on Pluto do times tables and spelling tests. And the thing that escaped and became giant is still on the loose. But tell PresiJim Grandad to enjoy his holiday. Everything is fine and <u>completely</u> normal.

For Pluto.

Jon x

Gran Fisher-Clyde

Flabber Flotel

Ring Street

D Ring

Saturn

Doolyboppers

Pluto

Dear Mum,

Any luck catching
the beast? The Snargler Spotters'
Society is getting very excited.

Everyone is working hard on their
penpal letters. Everyone except
Straxi and me. I told Mrs Hall we
don't need to write to each other
anymore because I'm writing to you
now. Also Straxi and I are both here

on Pluto. "That's no excuse," said Mrs Hall.

Bryd finally managed to spell Opuntia Microdasys and finish her letter. Now she just has to write the envelope.

On the way home from school, it was really dark and grey. I thought the Dome lights had gone wrong again but then we saw the Dome Cleaners all sitting round looking stressed and testing each other on maths questions instead of squirting the walls clean.

When we got back to Doolyboppers,

there weren't any Whirlywangs as

Straxi's mum was doing a spelling

test.

No Whirlywangs?

What is happening to Pluto?

Love Jon

Dear Straxi,

Please pass the yuffs.

Yours sincerely,
Jon

Dear Jon,

What?

Yours faithfully with glittery bits,
Straxi

Dear Straxi,

You heard. <u>Yuffs!</u>

Yours extra loudly,
Jon

Dear Jon,

Too late, I've eaten them.

Yours in fullness,
Straxi

Northcroft Road

Earth

Dear Jon,

Dad and I got the box ready. We lined it with
comfy bedding and food. Now that Sparkly
Deathray is so big, we didn't think swamp mites
would be enough, even if we could see them to
find them, so Dad popped in a few loaves of
bread and some steaks. We took the box upstairs
and left it open with food inside, and then went
to open Jason's door.

"No! You're not taking Deathray!" yelled Jason,

blocking the door which was covered in posters saying 'Save the Snargler' and 'Deathray Belongs on Earth'.

"But Deathray doesn't belong on Earth, it belongs on Pluto," Dad explained.

"And it's called Sparkly," Jenny added.

"It's time to say goodbye, Jason," I said firmly.

Then we realised Jason had chained himself to the door. This may take some time.

Love Mum & Dad

Doolyboppers

Pluto

Dear Mum,

Try this.

Jon

Dear Jason's girlfriend,

It's Jon here, Jason's annoying little

brother.

At least, that's what he calls me but

really I'm <u>tons</u> less annoying than him

and better looking too — and I saved

Pluto from ~~eco~~ ~~ecology~~ natural disaster

so I'm sort of famous. Anyway, he is

also a Snargler Spotter who wears an

Northcroft Road

Earth

Dear Jon,

Sparkly Deathray is on its way!

I can't believe we managed it. Jason opened the door and it oozed straight out and into the box. It must have been starving. Or suffocating from Jason's crusty odd socks.

We had to use a bigger box again, by the way. We used the one the new garden shed came in.

D
L

"So long, Deathray. It's been real," Jason said, giving it a final blast of heavy metal music. What that poor creature has been through I dread to think.

"Goodbye Sparkly. I love you," Jenny said, sprinkling it with glitter and taping up the box with bright pink sticky tape.

"Air holes!" I shrieked, and quickly punched some in with a pencil.

We then looked through them to check Sparkly Deathray was still alive. I saw a fang so luckily it was.

Look out for a massive cardboard box coming to

Doolyboppers.

Love Mum & Dad

DANGER!

DO NOT OP

God luk
Sparkly

JON FIS
C/O DO

Doolyboppers

Pluto

Dear Mum,

Straxi, Bryd and I walked home from school and found a massive cardboard box outside Doolyboppers. There was a big hole in the side which was the size of a big bruv, e.g. huge. On the ground was an old sock and a pile of glitter.

Sparkly Deathray has escaped!!!

We ran to the nearest microphone on a stick at the side of the pavement to call for a Pluto Guardian. When he turned up he was an old one so he took ten minutes not five like they're supposed to, and when he saw the hole in the box he had to sit down for another ten minutes.

Then he called the Snargler Spotters' Society and they turned up in about two seconds and got out tape measures to measure the hole and made little notes in their notebooks and said Snargler 192 had mutated beyond anything they had ever seen before. They were very excited but also worried as who knows what Snargler 192 might do now it's huge and on the loose? I told them it was now called Sparkly Deathray but they pretended not to hear.

Then the Snargler Spotters asked the Pluto Guardian for help but he said there was no one else free as they all have to do a project on the Iron Age for Mrs Hall by next Friday.

"Don't worry," I said. "We will help. We saved Pluto before and we can do it again."

Bryd said she would stay at Doolyboppers in case Sparkly Deathray returns to its box.

Straxi and I are going to ask Mrs Urdlepun if we can borrow the class robot for the weekend. It will be an ADVENTURE.

Love Jon

Northcroft Road

Earth

Dear Jon,

Stop.

Remember what happened on your last Pluto
adventure.

Let the Pluto Guardians take care of things.
Why are they doing a project on the Iron Age
for Mrs Hall? I don't understand.

Here is another letter from Jenny to Fiona.

D
L

Now she misses Fiona <u>and</u> Sparkly Deathray.

And I hate to say this but here is a letter from Jason to Sparkly Deathray.

Love Mum & Dad

Dawn's Lawns jobs

✓ Trim lawn outside barber's - short back and sides?

✓ Design glow-in-the-dark garden for Insomniacs Anonymous

✓ Send back box of ~~100~~ 99 garden gnomes

- ~~Reorder Mrs Thompson's garden gnome~~

D
L

Dear Fiona the
Feathery Pony

Help you hav to find Sparkly
it has gon to Pluto it looks
like a sosage

DON'T EAT SPARKLY!

Luve from yor very best
frend

Jenny that's me

xxxxxxxxx

Dear Deathray,

You are awesome! Don't let them catch you and put you in a zoo.

And don't eat anyone. But if you do have to, my little bruv is on Pluto and would make a great snack.

I miss you a lot. You were the biggest snargler I ever saw and you earned me ⑤⓪ points in my Spotters' Notebook.

Respect,

Jason

Mimas

Jon,

You'll never guess – I'm through to the finals! Classic! Grandad President Jim is upgrading my Turbo-Charged NitroPod SE to a Limited Edition ThrustPod Supreme with anti-matter thrusters and go faster dice. Tasty!

Got to go – parachuting as I write and about to land (I hope)!

Gran x

Jon Fisher

c/o The Doolys

Doolyboppers

Dizzy Street

Dome 1

Pluto

Hi Gran,

Good luck in the finals.
The go faster dice will
help! The thing that escaped has
escaped back here but needs to
be unescaped and nobody can
find it. Everyone is too busy with
homework for Mrs Hall. But
Straxi and I are on the case.
I'm sure it will all be okay.

Jon x

Gran Fisher-

Clyde

Flabber Flotel

Ring Street

D Ring

Saturn

EVEN MORE NEW PLUTO LAWS

· Please raise your hand if you wish to speak to anyone.

· Walk down Main Street, don't run. Dropped takeaway Whirlywangs are not nice for others to step on.

· Compulsory show-and-tell will start this Fiveday in Blurble Park, where Boogle Bopton will show us his collection of shopping bags.

Signed Mrs Hall, Temporary President

PERMISSION SLIP

Student | Straxi Dooly and Jon Fisher

Class | 6U

Resource | Class Robot

Reason | Snargler spotting

Signed | Mrs Urdlepun

Don't wear out the batteries too much!

6U ROBOT REPORT

Date: 17.02.2318

1000 Switching on.

Environment: Human eating establishment called Doolyboppers.

Observation: Tall vases filled with sugary gunk called Whirlywangs being served.

Action: Play educational song 'Sugar Free Me' by Broccoli Spears to promote healthy eating. No one listens. Fade out and engage embarrassment circuits.

1030

Environment: Doolyboppers.

Observation: Students Straxi and Jon fill my storage area with following items:

1 nature notebook

1 low gravity pen

1 giant fishing net

1 family size bag of yuffs

Action: Overload warning light goes on. Student Straxi removes bag of yuffs, eats one and returns them. Overload warning light goes off. Ready to depart.

1100

Environment: Dizzy Street.

Observation: Students Straxi and Jon inform me of mission to rescue confused snargler.

Action: Enquire what could confuse snarglers who are simple, dull swamp-dwelling slugs. "Space travel," replies student Jon.

YUFFS

1130

Environment: Town square opposite statue of Flumpenslurp Blurble.

Observation: Students Straxi and Jon eat yuffs and reflect on progress of mission. No progress yet made. Many adult humans are building model Iron Age village from cereal boxes and furgel juice cartons.

Action: Play humorous educational video 'No More Creases in My Trousers — It's the Iron Age!' narrated by Tony Robotson. Watched by one person.

1200

Environment: Town square.

Observation: Herd of blue-headed skwitches arrive and step on model Iron Age village. Cries of rage and frustration from adult humans. Skwitches leave, satisfied with their work.

1230

Environment: Main Street.

Observation: Mission has been resumed.

1300

Environment: Main Street.

Observation: Students Straxi and Jon stop for another break. Finish yuffs.

1330

Environment: Main Street.

Observation: Students Straxi and Jon stop to check if yuffs definitely finished. Affirmative.

1400

Environment: Blue Prairies Trail.

Observations: Student Jon comments that neither he nor student Straxi remembered to bring a drink.

1430

Environment: Blue Prairies Trail.

Observation: Student Jon comments that all he can think about is water.

1500

Environment: Blue Prairies Trail.

Observation: Student Jon drags himself along the ground gasping, "Water! Water!"

1600

Environment: Town Square.

Action: Visit furgel juice bar. Also purchase more yuffs.

1630

Environment: Blue Prairies Trail.

Observation: Students Straxi and Jon finish yuffs.

1730

Environment: Pulsating Swamp.

Action: Play students educational musical video 'Pulsating Swamp, the Third Wonder of Pluto' with music by Android Webber.

Observation: Students fall asleep.

1800
Environment: Pulsating Swamp.
Action: Wake up students.

1830
Environment: Pulsating Swamp.
Action: Begin to search area.

1900
Environment: Pulsating Swamp.
Observation: Dome lights go out.
Action: Leave Pulsating Swamp and return
to base.

1930 Switching off.

6U ROBOT REPORT   Date: 18.02.2318

1000   Switching on.
Environment: Doolyboppers.
Observation: Consult memory chip and
confirm this is day 2 of mission to rescue
confused snargler with students Straxi and
Jon.
Action: Try to switch off again.
Additional observation: Remember student
Straxi has remote control.

1030
Environment: Doolyboppers.
Observation: Given Whirlywang for breakfast.
Apparently a 'joke'.
Action: Engage laughter circuits. Ha. Ha. Ha.

1100

Environment: Dizzy Street.

Observation: "No yuff breaks. This time we mean business," says student Straxi.

Action: Engage doubtfulness circuits.

1130

Environment: Main Street.

Observation: Without supply of yuffs, students Straxi and Jon have exhausted their power supplies. I have not. They make plan.

Action: Activate concern circuits.

1200

Environment: Pulsating Swamp.

Observation: I am carrying students Straxi and Jon. I am not designed to support

weight of 2 students. Or any students.
Action: Play educational video 'How to
Conserve the Energy of Your Class Robot'
with extra sound effects, light show and
holograms. Oops.

1200
Environment: Pulsating Swamp.
Observation: Power running low. Switch to
auto pilot. Now can only say 'Yes' or 'No'
or play the greatest hits of Android
Webber and Tin Rice.
Action: Switching off.

1700
Switching on.
Environment: Doolyboppers.

Observation: Batteries on emergency power. Six-foot bird feather stuck in my back wheel. Student Straxi explains I was flown home on back of blue-headed skwitch. I am not designed to fly on back of blue-headed skwitch.

Action: Shock has drained the last of my batteries. Switching off.

Snargler Spotters' Society

SPECIAL EMERGENCY BULLETIN

Oneday 19 Fiennes 2318

Dear members,

Thank you to everyone who volunteered to carry buckets of Pulsating Swamp water over to the Glowing Canyon, and for those who brought flasks of plubberslurp to keep everyone going.

We now have a large and safe environment for this magnificent creature and can only hope it Is attracted to the muddy brown sludge as it is too huge and mutated for us to catch.

Eugene Nerdlington, Chief Snargler Spotter

Doolyboppers

Pluto

Dear Mum,

We didn't find Sparkly Deathray. And
we were banned from borrowing the
class robot ever again.

Apart from that it was a ⌐brilliant⌐
mission and we got lost and flew home

on a skwitch! I
think it was
Armitage Shanks
and he didn't even try

to kidnap us this time either.

Straxi's gran said why don't we make some posters instead, and she is the head teacher of Flumpenslurp Blurble School so we had to say yes.

We have put them up everywhere. Straxi said the Snargler Spotters' Society will probably make me a Gold Member just like her for all the work I've put in, so I took a few posters down just in case.

Jon

Northcroft Road

Earth

Dear Jon,

I hope you are safe. I feel so terrible sending
Sparkly Deathray to wreak havoc on Pluto. Maybe
it will shrink down to normal size now it's back in
its proper home?

We had an interesting delivery today: it was your
lunch box. The school sent it over on the end of
a crane and dropped it into the garden. I went
to pick it up but the driver, who was wearing a
biohazard suit, said it was best to leave a

'buffer zone' around it. I think I will.

Dad also had an interesting day as he took three computers apart to mend them and ended up with one. Dad said the customer loved their new super computer but the other two customers weren't very happy.

I'm glad you've found another way of searching for Sparkly Deathray. Jason and Jenny soon cheered up. Jenny has dressed Jason up as a giant snargler and he is chasing her. It makes them both very happy.

Love Mum & Dad

YET MORE NEW
PLUTO LAWS

• All citizens are advised to stay inside their classrooms - I mean, homes - until further notice.

• This is an ideal time to finish your Iron Age projects and revise for next week's spelling test.

• As I am worried about going outside myself, I have stuck this poster to the inside of my hotel room window.

signed Mrs Hall, Temporary President

Doolyboppers

Pluto

Dear Mum,

After our poster campaign, no one
will go out and look for Sparkly
Deathray as they are now terrified.

In fact, no one's going out at all.
The most recent sighting was by
Boogle Bopton who said that Sparkly
Deathray is now the size of a double-
decker hoverbus.

hoverbus

Sparkly

Bryd said maybe we should deliver
Blobble Burgers to everyone, but Mr
Dooly said, "After you then, Bryd!" and
Bryd looked at the poster we made
of Sparkly Deathray and said actually
no thanks.

Then Straxi said she would go and Mr
and Mrs Dooly said no way. So we all
sat inside and looked out of the
window at the empty street. I could
see all the way to Flumpenslurp
Blurble School which we can't go to
because it's too dangerous with a
deranged snargler on the loose.

"I wonder if Mrs Hall is enjoying being in charge of Pluto," I said, and then Straxi came up with a brilliant idea and said, "Let's write to her and get her to do something."

And then I had an even better idea.

It's going to start with writing a letter to everyone on Pluto.

Love Jon

Dear Pluto people,

Please do not freak out at the ten-
foot bird that is delivering this letter.
We have a much bigger problem: the
giant snargler on the loose.

If we all write to Mrs Hall maybe she
will change the new Pluto rules and we
can all work together to catch
Sparkly Deathray. Please attach your
letter to this skwitch.

Jon Fisher

Dear Mrs Hall,

I'm a swamp guide and I love snarglers but having a huge, giant, scary one is putting people off coming to the Pulsating Swamp. I'd be happy to help catch it if I had some assistance and didn't have to master my seven times table at the same time, which is the trickiest one for me personally.

Fnorf Axminster, Pulsating Swamp assistant

Dear Mrs Hall

Please can I hand my essay about what I did over my summer holiday in to you late so I can help catch the giant snargler?

Stella Spinnington, Pluto Guardian

Hey Mrs H,

Catching a monster would be totally cool!

Count us in.

Love from the Gravity Guys

Dear Marion,

Dome 1 is the friendliest place on Pluto, but not with a giant snargler about. I would love to help catch it although I may not finish my Iron Age roundhouse in time.

Boogle Bopton, friendly folk

Dear Mrs Hall,

As a Pluff I am always happy to do more Pluffing, and if that helps me get extra golden time then even better.

Purton Yeargold, Pluff

Jon,

Well, I did my best. It's the taking part that counts. Only joking —

I WON!!!

Coolio! It was a tough race and I nearly came off the outer ring at one point but the anti-matter thrusters kicked in just in time.

Got to go — doing a victory lap!

Gran x

Jon Fisher

c/o The Doolys

Doolyboppers

Dizzy Street

Dome 1

Pluto

Atlas

Hi Gran,

Yay! I knew you could do it!
The thing that escaped has now
come back as a monster and
the streets are empty. But don't
worry. Maybe that happens all
the time on Pluto. And Straxi
and I are bound to
come up with
another plan.

Jon x

Gran Fisher-Clyde

Flabber Flotel

Ring Street

D Ring

Saturn

Straxi, how are we going to get all the letters delivered to Mrs Hall? Fiona the FP has flown off again and the postman was chased by Sparkly Deathray into Dome 2 and won't come out.

- Jon

I have a plan.
- Straxi

Let me guess. Does it involve dressing up as snarglers? Because Mum and Dad still have the costumes.
- Jon

No.

– Straxi

phew.

– Jon

It involves dressing up as skwitches. Because if there's one thing a snargler is afraid of, it's a skwitch. They don't eat them or anything. They're just freaked out by their extra long legs.

– Straxi

All right, if we have to. So we dress up as Fiona and Armitage, right?

– Jon

We are too small to be Fiona and Armitage. We will have to be Fiona OR Armitage. I vote for Fiona. I will sit on your shoulders. I have the skwitch costume but you will need black tights and flippers.
- Straxi

I should have known. Alright. I can see the flippers from here. <u>Let's go.</u>
- Jon

Doolyboppers

Dizzy Street

Dome 1

Pluto

                         Threeday 28 Fiennes

Dear Mrs Hall

Here are lots of letters for you.

We've left them outside your hotel

room as they won't fit through the

letterbox and we don't want to be

outside any longer as we might get

eaten by Sparkly Deathray.

Please do something as you are the Temporary President.

From Jon

PS This letter should definitely win the school cactus because it got lots of other people writing too.

PPS I don't actually want the school cactus. I just want to win.

PPPS Who <u>would</u> want the school cactus?

Vertigo Hotel

Dome 1

Threeday 28 Fiennes 2318

Dear citizens of Pluto,

How wonderful to see you all writing letters!

Normally this would make me very pleased, except
for the fact that they are all complaining about a
rampaging monster let loose in our streets.

Thank you everyone for the offers of help. Perhaps I
have got a little carried away with running Pluto
and given you all rather too much to do. However,
this is my mess and I am determined to tackle it

single-handedly.

I have dealt with the likes of Jason Fisher and Rex Smith, and a mutated double-ended swamp creature is <u>not</u> going to defeat me.

I will simply explain to it the error of its ways and guide it back to the swamp in a controlled and calm manner.

Yours sincerely,
Mrs Hall

Doolyboppers

Pluto

Dear Mum,

Straxi and I delivered all the letters
to Mrs Hall. Then we headed back to
Doolyboppers.

It was weird with nobody around like
Friendly Folk and Skwitch Herders and
the odd Pluff. At least Straxi said it
was. I couldn't see anything as I was
in the bottom half of the skwitch
costume. All I could see out of my

eyeholes were my feet and
the odd zork.

"Where are we going?" I called,
but all that came out was, "Mm
mm mm mmmm?" as my voice was
muffled by feathers. At last I saw
grass under my feet — the blue grass
they have on Pluto — and I knew I
was in the Blue Prairies.

"Let's check Fiona and Armitage's
nest," said Straxi, but just then we
heard a giant rumble and the ground
started to shake.

"It's Sparkly!" I yelled, but all that came out was, "Mm mmmm mm mm!"

The rumbling got louder and louder and suddenly I could feel hot, rancid breath coming through my eyeholes.

<u>**We're doomed!**</u> I thought, but then the ground zoomed away from me at a hundred miles an hour, the skwitch costume fell off in mid air and I found myself sitting in a pile of sticks. Straxi was next to me, grinning.

"Thanks Armitage!" she said.

Armitage Shanks was sitting next to us in the nest with his long legs dangling over the edge and the usual smug smile on his beak. I swear he enjoys putting me through this sort of thing.

We looked down (I could see now) and there was Sparkly Deathray charging across the Blue Prairies like a line of rampaging

elephants all very close together.
And there, on its back, was Mrs Hall.

"Jon! Meet us at the Glowing Canyon!
And bring some swamp water!" she
yelled, as she rode away and
disappeared from view.

I never thought I'd ever say this but,

just at that moment, Mrs Hall was
<u>pretty cool.</u>

"How are we going to do all that?" I
asked Straxi, who was already
climbing up onto Fiona's back.

"Oh no. Not again!" I said, as she
pushed me onto Armitage's back.
I hung on tight as Armitage stood up,
nearly tipping me off, and flapped his
freakily tiny wings before launching
himself into the air.

"Wahooooo!" shouted Straxi.

- When we reached the Pulsating Swamp, the snargler spotters were so surprised they even stopped spotting snarglers for a bit. When we explained why we were there, they immediately gave us two big buckets of swamp water and told us they would bring more as soon as they had put their notebooks away.

- Flying on a blue-headed skwitch carrying a bucket of swamp water is pretty tricky, but when I saw Mrs Hall

riding round and round the Glowing
Canyon on a giant mutated snargler I
realised it was probably quite easy in
comparison.

We chucked the swamp water into
the canyon and Sparkly instantly
zoomed towards it. Right at the last
minute, Mrs Hall slid off and Sparkly
leapt into the canyon with a big splash
of slime.

"That was amazing, Mrs Hall," I told
her.

"Didn't I ever mention I'm the three-time winner of the Robotic Rhino Rodeo?" said Mrs Hall, her eyes sparkling with excitement or possibly slime.

WOWSERS

Love Jon

PS When we were in Fiona and Armitage's nest there were six massive eggs inside!

NEW PLUTO LAWS

• Today is a holiday. Free Whirlywangs at Doolyboppers are on me!

• All previous laws are no longer in force. (Apart from the laws you had originally. They still apply.)

• And detention for dropping litter.

• And please continue to write to your penpals. They'd like that.

Mrs Hall, Temporary President

Dear Bryd,

I won this for writing the best letter.

But I think you should have it.

Love Jon

Jon,

You'll never guess what the prize was for winning the Saturn Ring Race. A brand new ElectroPod 3000 VT with blacked out windows and supernova throttle! Sweet!

By the way, Grandad President Jim has found lots more of your postcards under the floating doormat of our Flotel room. Just going to read them all now.

Gran x

Jon Fisher

c/o The Doolys

Doolyboppers

Dizzy Street

Dome 1

Pluto

Pandora

URGENT

SUPER HIGH
SPEED SHUTTLE

Methone

Jon Fisher
c/o The Doolys
Doolyboppers
Dizzy Street
Dome 1
Pluto

URGENT

Jon,

Have read the letters.
On our way!

Gran x

WELCOME HOME PRESIDENT JIM AND DORIS!
WE HAVE MISSED YOU!
From the citizens of Pluto

WELCOME TO YOUR NEW HOME SNARGLER 192!
WE HAVE MISSED YOU!
From all at the Snargler Spotters' Society

SPECIAL EMERGENCY BULLETIN

Fiveday 2 Mukherjee 2318

Dear members,

I am sure you will agree that Mrs Hall has performed a great service for the snargler community, and so I am delighted to announce that she has been awarded an honorary lifetime Gold Membership of the Snargler Spotters' Society.

A ceremony will be held next Funday at the clubhouse where I will present her with her anorak, membership certificate and, of course, notebook.

Eugene Nerdlington, Chief Snargler Spotter

Vertigo Hotel

Dome 1

Happyday 3 Mukherjee 2318

Dear Jon,

It has been an interesting challenge running Pluto, to say the least, but now the President is home I am turning my attention back to my Handwriting Campaign.

I have been invited by the Solar Education Committee to tour the planets spreading the message of letter writing, and I would like to take you along as the 'face' of my campaign.

I have already contacted your parents who both said you would be delighted to accompany me on my trip – indeed, they seemed thrilled that your journey would be extended, as of course I'm sure you are.

We will be leaving Pluto in a week's time. First stop, Neptune!

Best wishes,

Mrs Hall

SOLAR
education committee
Shining a light on learning

We invite you to tour round our solar system to spread the message of letter writing to everyone.

The trip will begin on Neptu...
Marion Hall's unique...

Doolyboppers

Dizzy Street

Dome 1

Funday 4 Mukherjee

Dear Mrs Hall

Mrs Urdlepun said you sent me a

letter. But I haven't got it so I don't

know what it says.

And I can't go. I'm an uncle now.

I have <u>responsibilities.</u>

From Jon

Vertigo Hotel

Dome 1

Oneday 5 Mukherjee 2318

Dear Jon,

Nonsense. See you at the spaceport next week.

Mrs Hall

WHOOSH

SINGLE TICKET TO
NEPTUNE
JON FISHER

We Help Org
Outer Space Ho

Spaceship: Spacey McSpa
Captain: Timothy Peake X
Voyage: 1 Day
Distance: 4.5 billion km

Straxi,

If you find this note it means I've gone to live with the snarglers. Anything is better than going round the solar system with Mrs Hall.

Jon

Jon,

I am making you a snargler costume as I write.

Good luck!

Straxi

Northcroft Road

Earth

Dear Jon,

So relieved that Sparkly Deathray has a proper
home at last! And did you hear that Gran won
her race?

Mrs Hall says you haven't received a letter she
sent to you, which is strange as apparently she
posted it through your door, so on your behalf we
have accepted her offer to take you round the
Solar System dressed as a giant pencil.

Enjoy the trip and don't forget to write.

Dad says you can use yourself, ha ha!

Love Mum & Dad

PS I am sending you a new toothbrush. It comes

on a cord so you can wear it round your neck

and never forget to brush your teeth ever again.

You will remember, won't you?

Dawn's Lawns jobs

✔ Cut corners of lawn for Time
    Savers' Society

✔ Trim hedge funds at bank

✔ Deliver Mrs Thompson's garden ~~gnome~~ dome!!!
    keep

✔ ~~Send back~~ garden gnome

Straxi,

Don't worry about the costume.
Apparently I already have one.

It's a pencil.

Please write to me.

I'll be on Neptune.

And send help.

Jon

Vomblefruit tre

So cute!!!

A rare moment of relaxation

THE SOLAR TIMES

Pluto edition

Max 26C, min 9C   12 Mukherjee 2318   1 plound

SKWITCH BABIES

Our Dome 1 skwitch herder is delighted to announce the birth of six new blue-headed skwitches at the new nesting site/modern art sculpture park design-ed by Flip Dooly. Visitors are being asked to keep away and leave the babies in peace, although this has been difficult to achieve.

"I'm not leaving," said Straxi Dooly, whose father won the compet-ition to design the nesting site.

"I'm going to be a skwitch when I grow up anyway."

The parents of the new babies, Straxi told the Solar Times, are called Armitage Shanks and Fiona the Feathery Pony. She will be naming the babies shortly.

TEACHER ADMITS SHE WAS 'A LITTLE OVER THE TOP'

Mrs Hall, our recent temporary president, admitted yesterday that she may have gone "a little over the top" in her recent custodianship of Pluto.

"Spelling tests and times tables every day were a good idea, but the assemblies were very poorly attended and some people didn't even care about missing golden time."

Would she do it again? "No." Fair enough.

"But only because I'll be travelling the solar system promoting my handwriting campaign. I can always come back again afterwards." We wished her a long and pleasant, but mostly long, trip.

PRESIDENT RETURNS

All of Pluto turned out to welcome President Jim and his new wife Doris back from their honeymoon, as they touched down at the space port in an ElectroPod 3000 VT with blacked out windows and supernova throttle, rated 'Best Pod of the Year' by Top Pod Magazine.

The President was eager to get back to work and has already planned some more competitions, starting with designing the plumbing for the town hall.

Meanwhile Doris is looking forward to more travels in the ElectroPod. "The solar system is my lobster!" she chortled.

GIRL WRITES TO PLANT

In a recent penpal writing programme at Flumpenslurp Blurble School, pupil Bryd Dooly discovered she was actually writing to a cactus. "I wondered why Opuntia Microdasys wasn't writing back," said Bryd.

Her penpal turned out to be a plant which was brought to Earth by Mrs Hall, the temporary President of Pluto. Bryd has now decided to teach Opuntia how to write. "I'm very patient. I'll sta_ with bedtime stories _ soon pick it up.

The End

141

PLANET-HOPPING
PENSIONERS
MONTHLY
INSIDE:
Meet our cover star:
Doris Fisher-Clyde!
Over 70 and still
on Earth?
Our top ten tips
for leaving terra firma
Deadly dangers -
the pros and cons of Neptune
Plus: win an anti-matter
zimmer frame. It's
cutting-edge cool!

WHY NOT VISIT THE GLOWING CANYON?

Marvel at the glowing rocks that make this place one of the SEVEN WONDERS of Pluto!

Enjoy the stunning views of the canyon!

And gasp at the size of the MUTANT SNARGLER that now lives here!

Please bring a bucket of swamp water. Collections can be made from the Pulsating Swamp. See Eugene Nerdlington for details.

If you enjoy visiting Snargler 192, why not join the new Giant Snargler Spotters' Society? We meet up to spot giant snarglers and write about them in our Giant Snargler Spotters' Notebooks. Free giant notebook for every member.

The President's Residence,

Main Street, Dome 1

Dear Straxi and Bryd's gran (or may I call you

Bev?),

I am planning a trip in my ElectroPod 3000 VT

and I wondered whether you would like to

accompany me? It will be a lovely trip with

beautiful views of scenic Neptune, where

I plan to get revenge on that blarb-ringed

flapper once and for all.

Doris

PS Bring your surfing gear. It will be rad.